BIG TOP
SCOOBY-DOO!™
MOVIE READER

adapted by Sonia Sander
Based upon the script written by Doug Langdale

WORLDWIDE PUBLISHING

SCHOLASTIC INC.

ISBN 978-0-545-45718-7

12 11 10 9 8 7 6 5 4 3 2 1   12 13 14 15 16 17/0

Designed by Henry W. Ng
Printed in the U.S.A.   40
First printing, August 2012

The kids from Mystery Inc. were on vacation in Atlantic City. "What should we do first?" asked Daphne.

"Let's go see Wulfsmooon!" sang Shaggy, pointing at a sign above. "They're only, like, the best rock band ever!"

"No, we have to go to the circus!" said Fred.

"Looks like they don't even open until tomorrow night," said Shaggy.

"Hang on," said Fred. "The door is open. Let's take a look inside."

The circus was dark and full of shadows.

"On a creepy scale, this ranks higher than a graveyard," said Shaggy.

That's when a shadow jumped out at them!
Luckily, it was only Marius, the circus owner.
When Fred told him the door was open, Marius
was very upset.

"Come, we must stick together," said Marius.
"I am sure that jewel-stealing werewolf is here."

"Rererolf?" cried Scooby. "Rikes!"

While the gang was looking for the werewolf, Shaggy and Scooby stopped at the baboon cage. Scooby made funny faces, and the baboons copied him.

Shaggy made faces, too, and the baboons cowered in fear.

"Sorry, baboon-dudes, I didn't mean to scare you," said Shaggy.

But it wasn't Shaggy that scared the baboons. It was the werewolf!

Scooby and Shaggy ran away.

After they lost the werewolf, Marius took Scooby and the gang back to his office.

"My uncle gave me this circus," he told them. "I think the werewolf may be an unhappy troupe member. He's followed us around, scaring people and stealing jewelry."

"I remember a case from a hundred years ago," said Velma. "Instead of waiting for a full moon, this werewolf used precious stones to change any time he wanted."

"Marius, let us help you catch the werewolf," said Fred. "We'll dress up as circus performers!"

That night, Scooby and Shaggy headed
out to look for dinner. But instead of
food, they found the werewolf!

"When I say so, run!" cried Shaggy.

Scooby didn't wait. He raced into a
nearby museum.

Inside, Shaggy and Scooby found an injured security guard. They also saw the werewolf steal a jeweled necklace.

"Like, how did it get in here so fast?" asked Shaggy.

The two friends raced back outside. There they ran into Fred, Daphne, and Velma.

All of the sudden, a werewolf in clown clothes jumped on top of the Mystery Machine.

"Hold on! There are two werewolves now?" asked Fred.

"That one's wearing Schmatko's costume. He must have gotten bitten!" cried Daphne.

"Like, RUN!" cried Shaggy.

The gang managed to escape from the two werewolves.

The next morning, Daphne discovered an old book in Marius's office.

"This book is all about the werewolf from a hundred years ago," said Velma. "Someone has circled all the jewels needed to transform into a werewolf except for one, the carbonado."

Velma did some research. She discovered that a carbonado was a black diamond.

Marius told the gang the circus was doing a special show just for Wulfsmooon.

"Zoinks! Like, their lead singer, Wulfric, wears a black diamond!" cried Shaggy.

Velma thought Marius was the werewolf. She was sure he wanted Wulfric's diamond!

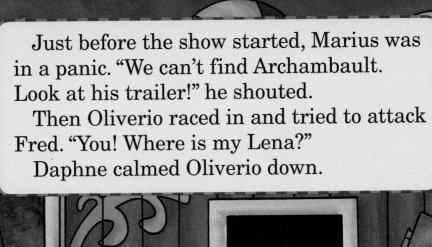

Just before the show started, Marius was in a panic. "We can't find Archambault. Look at his trailer!" he shouted.

Then Oliverio raced in and tried to attack Fred. "You! Where is my Lena?"

Daphne calmed Oliverio down.

Just before the show, Marius went missing, too.

"The show must go on!" Fred declared. As soon as the circus started, a werewolf attacked Wulfric. Daphne lassoed a second werewolf from her motorbike.

But now there were five werewolves to fight!

As Shaggy tried to stop a werewolf, he tore off some fur. Underneath was red fur — just like the baboons!

The baboons' cage was empty. "Raggy, raboons!" Scooby barked.

"Zoinks! The animal trainer must be behind this," said Shaggy. "Like, what was that command Doubleday used?"

"Descanso!" As soon as Shaggy used the command, the werewolf sat still.

The command worked on most of the werewolves, but one was escaping!

Velma knew what to do. She climbed into the cannon and yelled, "Fire, Fred!"

THUD! Velma hit the werewolf.

Velma ripped off the werewolf's mask. It was Doubleday, the animal trainer! He tried to escape, but Archambault came and shot him with a tranquilizer.

"We were all locked up in a storage shed out back. It took me hours to break out of these ropes," said Archambault.

Soon, the police arrived and took Doubleday away.

"Where's my amulet?" asked Wulfric.

"I've got officers looking for it," said the police chief.

The next morning, the gang said good-bye to Marius, Archambault, and the clowns.

"Thank you for all your help," said Marius. "Good-bye!"

"Farewell," Archambault said. "I hope the police find the black diamond."

"Another case solved," said Fred.

"Something isn't right," said Velma. "How did Archambault know it was a black diamond?"

"You're right, Velma!" Daphne cried. "Archambault's ropes weren't even broken. They were cut. He must have been in on it, too. We've got to catch that train!"

Scooby and Shaggy sneaked onboard the train. Marius and Archambault were fighting!

The two buddies knew they had to do something. So Scooby asked the circus animals for help.

While the baboons attacked, Shaggy
stole Archambault's tranquilizer darts
and the loot. Then Scooby and Shaggy
escaped through the roof of the train car.
But Archambault wasn't giving up
that easily. He followed them.

Archambault chased Scooby and Shaggy across one train car after another.

"Scoob, I've got an idea," cried Shaggy. "Follow me!"

Scooby and Shaggy jumped down between the train cars. When Archambault came after them, Shaggy threw all the tranquilizer darts at his nose. The strong man was out cold!

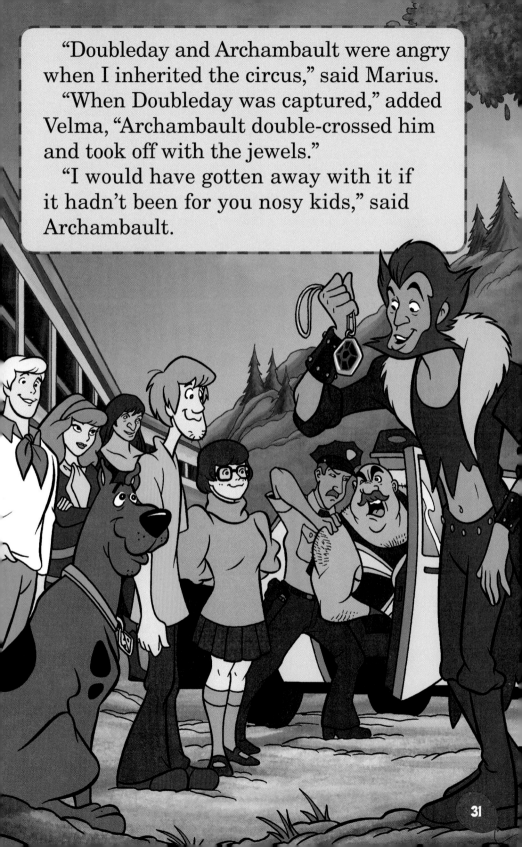

"Doubleday and Archambault were angry when I inherited the circus," said Marius.

"When Doubleday was captured," added Velma, "Archambault double-crossed him and took off with the jewels."

"I would have gotten away with it if it hadn't been for you nosy kids," said Archambault.

That night, Wulfsmooon thanked Scooby and the gang with a private concert.
Scooby-Dooby-Doo!